CW00835720

One of them Days

Zak Ferguson

Authors Note

One of them days is a book for one of them days where you're left agonising over your own mental health issues and intrusive thoughts, and you're left thinking, *I cannot cope, I cannot cope, I cannot cope, I cannot* fucking *cope...* And you are in dire need of a distraction.

A lot of people cannot cope with other people's issues, as it seems to lure their own out. Other times, escapism through art, that seems to tackle themes, issues, that you also suffer from, is quite therapeutic. Also, relatively reassuring.

The stories here are a varied few, where I have dealt with my own issues, fears, compulsions, and thoughts, in the only way I can, by writing about them. Fictionally, of course.

Well, this book is for you. Nothing helps someone better than experiencing, witnessing, someone else's suffering, and reading their work, that stems from their own mental health or neurological condition.

Also, why the f*ck not just suffer somebody else's mania and obsessive-compulsive issues, in book form? This is that book. This is that. Bask in it, and feel reassured, I am as fucked up, crazed and lonely, and at a loss as you are dear reader. Also, it is one of them days, every day.

– Zak Ferguson

" The pain you feel today is the strength you feel tomorrow. For every challenge encountered there is opportunity for growth."
— *Anonymous*

" You need to have a bad day once in a while, otherwise, you'll never know what a good day feels like."
— *Anonymous*

" I have no words to describe this day. I do, however, have a ton of obscene gestures."
— *Anonymous*

" Some days, the supply of available curse words is insufficient to meet my demands."
— *Anonymous*

1. One of them days, *for Stanley, concerning benefits and the other voice in his head.*

One of them days, I suppose. Yeah, one of those days. The sun is pissing me off. The hum of my refrigerator is getting under my skin.

It's one of them days, you know?

Where I am down on myself.

When *am I not* down on myself?

I am always down.

But there is always something that triggers it.

Today I got a letter from the DWP, Job-Centre-Plus – those goons that dictate my life, as to what amount I deserve, and I am expected to live off.

THAT I SHOULD LIVE OFF!

Mate, it is so difficult to carry across how I cannot be on JSA to them. Behind their *oh so* superior desks.

I am incapable of working, so, what makes them think I am capable of looking for work, just to satisfy them, or their algorithms, that I've looked hard enough? Strolling online, when I have no internet connection where I live, and my Giff-Gaff data charge is going on the up and up, and I have no petty cash to enable me their UNLIMITED DATA service. At least it isn't a standing order or repeat bill and I have the option to come and go as I please with their ever-changing data services and charges. I can barely afford their 5 quid one.

No money for internet. Not allowed in the local library, as I have lost my shit on the staff members, and the other Job Seeker Losers' far too many times to count off my fat fuck fingers.

I was on their probation list, where the local library gives you the, not three, but five strikes then you're out – rule.

What they do not tell you, nor offer in small non-existent print on their non-existent Library Tenancy Agreement that after the fifth, you're put on the neighbourhood watch list, and you're blacklisted everywhere.

They even go as far to tell the local internet cafes, that we have to pay to use, not to let you in, due to your outbursts and infuriated ways.

Their Terms and Agreements for usage that fail to notify you that -   where we are allotted 35 fucking minutes on their shoddy as fuck computers - that will take fifteen minutes to start up, eight more cunting minutes to get some form of connection. . . so you're left, with what? 12 minutes left.

23 minutes later you're faced with the JOB CENTRE PLUS website, thankful for small mercies, as thank god they do not have Vivaldi playing as background music for their site, otherwise I might actually have reason to be blacklisted from such places - is crashing, because every other youth in these environments, all as bedraggled, looks like shit-lookalike-muggins of whom are occupying the computers are struggling with the same lot in life as me.

I bet they have fast data and unlimited resources, lazy youthful drug dealing cunts that they all are. Living in some YMCA or FOYER property.

Wankers. The lot of them. Me, I am too, but I ain't that shameless.

I struggle to get up out of bed most days, and struggle to look at myself.

I am Stan the Man. Was. Were. If and when is another thing altogether.

Once upon a time, that is, I was Stan the Man. Gypo blood, with Gypo fists.

And when I do, well, you know, feel it, my old hey-hey-its-Stan-the-man-Day, heyday vibes and gut feeling, it is between 10:00 pm to 12am.

After a tinnie or ten.

Then I am left chain-smoking, waiting for the next thing to bother me.

 I go online, scroll through.

 Ain't updated my PROFILE Picture since I lost my job. Gotten fat and to post a recent photo, it is easy to see where one has gone. I have put on 8 stone. Fat is the new sign of being poor.

I go online, when I can, or when I can nick some Wiffy-signal from the local café down the road from my gaff, my inclination ain't to go on the Job Centre site, but to go onto social media. FB to be exact, and hunt down exes, old friends.

 They usually offset me. That and upset me.

I always look back in those days as, **THE DAYS,** of old, of me, Stan the Man.

When, actually, faced with these people, it bugs me.

They have more than me.

They have grown up.

They are better, brighter people.

Richer? Not in pocket but perhaps in their vain egotistical souls.

Leaning on a car that is a Merc and knowing fully well they're struggling to pay it off, on finance, but still have the gull to pass it off as just another one of the offshoots of their *oh so perfect* fucking existence.

Whilst I am still bitter and holding on for dear fucking life, on this raft known as nostalgia.

 A nostalgia for a time that was all fucking fake to begin with. That hurts, Bruv. That really stings me where it shouldn't.

Will it be, today, my breakdown, my weeping, my tempered dick pounding, to nasty ass faux-incest porn videos – coming from the real world or the imagined obsessive world I know we all occupy up top, that will offset me?

Well, got a letter I did, through my postbox. Letterbox. Fuck your box!

Fuckers do know how to ruin your letters, round 'ere. They shoved it in as if struggling to push a newborn calf back into its mother's cow-cunt.

Divvy cunts.

I get up early, to make that dreaded call. To explain my situation, and I am in fear of the results.

My excuse making (that most of them imply with their shit-don't-stink attitude, that is evident in their manner and poise – even though half my engagement is always down the bleeding hooter, I know they are being judgmental cunts) my reasoning as to why I am so behind looking for jobs.

 I AM NOT ON THE RIGHT BENEFITS.

How many fucking times do I have to tell 'em.

All because I've managed to hold down a job for at least fifteen years of my life, so they, the Job Centre lot, they expect me to have that - what is it? - that skill, and mindset, ready and in wait to be pushed upon and reapplied to my messed-up life.

I call them at 8:00 am.

Can't get through.

Electronic voice offers me an apology.

If she were a person, I would pity-fuck the broad.

When I do, I hear that music. SPRING, I think, by some famous, long forgotten, and unpaid in royalty cheques maestro.

Vivaldi.

Only know this as with my remaining data on my phone, I looked it up, to see what poor cunt has to have his supposed tour de force piece of music applied to something like the JOB CENTRE Plus phone line.

Wait line. What an awful fucking thing to do, to such a respected piece of music. Domain free is it?

Wouldn't have a song like Kanye's Black Jesus playing on loop, would you?

 Nah, 'cause that beat makes even the most even-tempered geezer - listening to it for pure musical entertainment - want to end up shivving people under their ribcage.

Imagine on the phoneline, if you are a mentally retarded and disturbed person (or persons, if you are that fucking nutty)- this tune playing, or something by some screamo heavy metal band?

The taxpayers wouldn't have to pay out so much no more for these daft cunts, who only need a little loud, thrumming music, to motivate them to kill each other off in some frenzied, non-politicised, all angry-fied spree.

Poor sod. That Vivaldi- guy!

Even in death his work isn't being used appropriately. Look, it ain't sonorous. That's the word, ain't it. Fuck. Me.

It ain't uplifting, it is repetitive and soul crushing.

You may think you are on the straight and narrow, and mentally able, after ten minutes on hold and listening to this loop of a "song", "tune" "classical orchestral piece" - well, after, you'll be half the man you were.

Think you were depressed to begin with, hahaha, well think again matey's - that usage of that tune will ensure you're a suicidal wreak like myself.

As I wait, breaking out of that tune, that theme of so many job seeker plus- supposed- nitwits, and benefit abusers- a voice reaches out, so I try a simple - "Hello?" instead of my usual "Uh!"

Nada. NUFFINK. Nothing, but the DAH-Dadada-Dah-Der-Dah! Da-Dah-Der-Dur-Da-dah-der-da-da-derh- da-derghhh-derghhh-derh!

Then it comes through.

I'm not that troublesome am I?

Hello darkness my old friend! Come to taunt me again?

Hello Samuel, how you doing? Missed me? How long has it been?

A few days.

Think you may need to up those meds, hahaha, I am only messing with you. How have you been? Still up to your old tricks, of trying to evade me.

SILENCE

That's all it needs to be faced with. Do not argue. Do not engage, just acknowledge it, and let it pass by.

Hello. Sammy-boy? I ain't really all that much of a pain in your backside, am I?

Yup. You are.

I'm not that much of a pain, am I?

SILENCE

Helloooooooooooooooooooooooooooo........

Can we just get this over with?

Of course. With what, Sammy boy? That is your name isn't it? Sammy. Not Stan the Man. Stan the Deluded Man Titan. Gypo blood? Since when? Since your grandma passed wind in her caravan and said, "Proper gypo blood there!" What? I am just saying, though I am in here, I ain't really occupying that much of your time! Am I?

You know you are, and all you're doing is leading me into a false sense of...

OF SECURITY! I was literally about to say that! Well, I did, didn't I? – Hahaha, the way the world works in here, its, well . . . It's marvelous! Ain't it so? Ain't it just?

Yup.

Yup. Is that all you can say? Yup. Nothing else you want to add, in this fine conversation we're having. No? Shame.

I know what you're doing, and it isn't cute.

I never thought I was cute!

Whatever you think you are. . .
just get it over with already!

You not feeling, a little low in yourself? I know it isn't me, as I am here to steer those low moods. I am not here to create them, as that is your department.

I do not bring this onto myself, I don't, and you know that, it is you!

Me, me, me. You, too. Bruv ting. Touch my ding, a sling. Bad man, ain'tcha? Hoodlum Bruv. All to fit into the environment you so love. NAWT! Hilarious this, the voice in your head, that isn't a voice, but is actually yourself. Projected, but, in a mental kind of way! I cannot be epitomized even of that, but can be viewed as your conscience of, not everything, but the isolated conscience born from your obsessive-compulsive mind! You have no clue what all my big, big, boy words mean? Do you?

I must do, how otherwise are they in me head?

Ooooo, smart-alecky, you being a smarty pants today? Huh? Fat cunt! Here! I didn't say cunt, I meant...Mary Hunt! I am not the sum and total of them all, these emotions, moods, fears, anxieties, and intrusive thoughts. I am just here to. . . rationalise, the irrational.

Please, just get this over with, please, please, please, please, please, please, P L E A S E !

Cut yourself much recently? Stan the Man, cut yourself? Dragged those knuckles across brick walls to make yourself look tougher, aye?! No. Shame. Imagine, if you could, like, cut open, the line, above your pubis, and fold over all that fat that is hiding your, lets me honest, small dick as it is, and you can pick at it, like sugar cubes and watch it dissolve. As much as you used to exercise and work out, and your pubis got slimmer and slimmer, you still had a wormy looking cock. Not been as much of a relief, hurting yourself, because you know that pain is gain and all you been gain fat boy is the pounds. Bad lifestyle. Chain-smoking, being morbidly obese, overall undesirable. You actually think I will go with death? Our thoughts are what makes us human. Our thoughts are our essence, Our soul. I am coming with you. Under the train tracks...or around the train tracks, as you will explode like a water balloon, but instead of water, full of human gunk.

Fuck you.

So, maybe, upon that slicing, and that release all you, cut and slicer types do and get a weird kick out of, what comes of it? Mess. And looking like a pussy because you cant do it. The real thing. Also, surface wound? Flesh wound? It is pitiful and a cry for help. Attention seeking. No manner of excuses will excuse your lame-ass existence and your need to cut in deep.

Piss off, alright just fuck off!
LEAVE ME ALONE!

"Thank you for waiting, we have ensured to react to your swearies, please continue to hold and we will answer your pitiful weeping and begging, in the form of a call, as soon as possible, you may prefer to call back later, or never, as our lines are open from 8am to 6pm Monday to Friday, for the desperate and the pitiful, and we are normally less busy between 8am and 9am, even though you have tried that, and we know, there has been no dice, so you may like to call back then…or NEVER"

Oh, for goodness sake.
This isn't funny.

I AM SORRY. . . I DIDN'T RECOGNISE THAT LAST NUMBER. . .that last, THOUGHT, THAT LAST OPTION… THAT LAST EXCUSE FOR YOUR LAZINESS… COULD YOU PLEASE REPEAT IT FOR ME? DID YOU SAY, INCOME AND SUPPORT ALLOWANCE? OR DID YOU SAY ESA. . .

Employment Support Allowance…OR DID YOU SAY, I AM A LOSER WHO CANNOT HOLD A JOB? HAHHAHAHAHA Vivaldi-Spring, Ha-along to it please whilst I Ha-Ha-Ha-a-ha-HA-Ha-Ha-a-ha-HA-Ha-HA-HA! **Do you know you're bleeding, Sam? Did you know that half of your nose has been crushed under the heavy blows you've inflicted upon it, and you have run red everywhere in your, mine, our, awful little Supported Accommodation Apartment?**

"Hello…this is Catherine, how may I take your call?"

"I-i-i-i-I'm…um…sorry…but I am *bleeding*"

"I'm sorry, I couldn't quite make out what you said. Hi, I am Catherine, how may I help you today?"

"I, need, help!"

"That is why I am here sir. To make things go quicker, could you, please, tell me your full name, date of birth or instead tell me your national insurance number"

"I don't think I want to carry on like this anymore…I'm sorry for what you're about to hear!"

She didn't hear anything, as she had ended this call, before I could scream down the phone at her.

It seems to be just one of those days.

Too fucking right. Also, your phone looks worse for fucking wear. You only smashed it into your head, you dumb fat fuck.

2. **One of them days,** *for Rupert and his nephews*

Rupert turns on his computer...and he begins to write. For a good few hours, he couldn't decide what font to use, as his eyesight wasn't as it used to be.

He was going to attempt to write it long hand, but after multiple attempts he stopped.

Arthritis was a bastard these days.

Sixty-five. Feeling like Eighty-five. Dead wife. No sons. One daughter. No clue where she was. Left age fourteen to be with some hippie who smoked the funny stuff. Only friends of his were Randall and Deirdre. Both him and his wife had met them on a holiday thirty years ago.

A few nephews, he treated like his own were a large part of both his and Maggie's life.

 Since Maggie's death, they haven't been as inclined to come over. Rupert couldn't blame them. They had to come over and bring their dear aunt down from the noose she had made for herself.

 Rupert shrunk into himself.

Could he do it?

Could he bring that sort of pain, back into their lives, so close to losing their Aunt Mags?

Rupert didn't know. Nor cared. He did. But not enough to stop him from typing this out. . .

I am not sad. I am just, tired. Tired. Lonely. Her death has left a deep impression in me. In the form of how I found her hanging from our ceiling, in the spare bedroom. I apologise for this font, it is the only font I can read properly. That or that comic sans, but it is ugly...

So, if you read this, and think, oh, you- soppy sod, you wanted to make it easy on us with the font style. I am sorry everyone but that wasn' t my intention and not much thought has gone into this really. Not unlike Mags.

Like everything she did she was always 110% behind it.

Her death was thought out.

I think she thought this would save me having to move into the spare bedroom, had she done it in our own, knowing I hated the spare-bed...

that she used to kick me out into after an argument, or most accurately, a barmy over my awful snoring.

Thoughtful as ever my lovely Maggie.

Also, she knew that if she killed herself in our room, and I decided to go into the spare, I would attempt to put our double in that single bed sized room.

Also, even in death I wouldn't have heard the end of it. The pointless task I would set about exacting. Like a lot of things, I did. It wasn't right. Nope. Not for my Mags. I miss you Mags.

I never fed into all that religious bullocks. But now, as I see the remainder, of my life ahead, however long, or short it is, I wish to be with yah me dear, my darling. So, what is there left to say but, I am going to hang myself in the living-room, as my favourite soaps theme tune drifts away with my own life. . .Mags, I am coming for you baby.

Rupert killed himself that very night. His seventh attempt that week. The suicide note was left at his feet, which were still swaying when his two nephews arrived.

Knocking gently, calling out for their "Unc Rupee!", as they walked the hallway, they got that feeling. The eldest of the two, Jamie rushed into the living-room, to the right of the hallway, and his youngest brother could hear the breath leave him as he entered.

Suddenly there was a lot of activity going on in the living-room, for all Tommy knew he could have been in a scuffle with their Uncle Rupert.

He was brought out of this thought when Jamie began screaming at the top of his lungs, *"TOMMY GET IN HERE...NOW...OH, YOU STUPID OLD GOAT...TOMMY WE CAN SAVE HIM! WE NEED TO GET HIM DOWN! TOMMY YOU TWAT HELP ME....Pleeeease, UNC Rupeee, wake up, Uncle Rupeee"*.

Tommy could hear their Uncle Rupee now, as they both tried to remain strong for him, who turned around, left to right, at each of them, during the funeral and said, "Save those tears. She knew what she was doing. Ballsy old bag she was".

They both should have known this was about to happen. But they just didn't let the thought cross their minds. Out of fear. Also, as respect to their Uncle. They respected their uncle and let him be. Allowing him to grieve in his own time and give him space, so as not to feel he had to keep up a front for them, the man that he was.

Occasionally over the past fourteen days, checking on over the telephone every evening, he seemed fine. Though distanced and sorrowful, he seemed up-beat, same old Uncle Rupee. But, with no accompaniment or voice behind him enquiring "Gives us the phone Rupee, I wanna talk to my boys!", that was another aspect of losing someone you love. The smallest of details become much more rounded and essential to your day-to-day life, the boys perhaps didn't call enough or try hard enough, due to their own grief.

The boys always ensured they both called together.

The last few calls, he seemed sated.

Almost as if something he had decided upon, that or had come to terms with, had lifted him a fraction.

Rupert was like a Father to the both of them, if not more, having stepped up to support his sister, having got knocked-up by some foreigner and buggered off back to whence he came, at the age of fifteen, and then history repeated itself not five years later when Tommy popped into this world wailing. Still, Rupert stuck by his sister's side. And raised the boys, with Maggie, as their own, alongside his sister. Never intervening. But there. A constant support, emotionally, financially when she struggled. She was a capable Mum, but just needed some extra support. And a reprieve.

How was their Mum going to take this?

They hadn't come over due to Rupert seeming to cut himself off the past few weeks, and obviously needing it. Wanting to be alone with his thoughts, and with, what he told them was, "The rest of my Mags soul" – so as they let themselves in with their spare key, they sensed a change.

As one rushed to get him down, check his vitals and to resuscitate, the other younger brother Tommy managed to get himself into the living-room, and spotted the note that had been crumpled partly by Jamie as he tried to lift his Uncle up, hoping the noose would slack and all of a sudden he would come to. Tommy picked up the printed note, still sticky and wet from the printer. On the back it read...

DO NOT RESUSCITATE. I WILL MAKE SURE MY NECK IS BROKEN...THIS TIME.

I love you lads, and also look after your bleeding Mother when I have gone. Love,
Unc Rupee. Xxx

As Jamie pumped, punched, and wept over his dead Uncle, Tommy laughed.

It was all he could do.

Was but laugh at the situation.

It seemed to be just one of them days.

3.
One of them Days. . . *For*
*Charlie-Daisy-Pop_Star1999 on her **blog***

Hey girls, oh and guys, Charlie_daisy- here today!

Gosh, it is one of those days. More jealous girls

picking on me at any chance they can get.

Calling me fat, and ugly, the usual go too's . . . ha

ha ha, I am not botherd. FACE BOTHER'd,

Catherine Tate is my Nanz favourite show as you all

now, .. oops, know…and so it is mine. People laugh and say, oh

"that is so 2005!!!!!" well guess what, I was born

in

2004, so shove that up your butt holes.

There is a game going on in school, called where

is the whale…they push scissors in the palm of

your hand, right into your palm and

wait, yup, wait for it, see how long you can last

before you waaaaillll, like a whale.

Apparently, I mean what noises does a wale make?

it sounds like a goat scream to me, from what I

heard come from Sonny-James Lintberg in the

girls' toilets. So much for being a bad ass smoker

boy type.

He got in deep doo-doo for that, funnily enough,

because he was in the girls' toilets, smoking and

pulling out his willy-winkle, I may only be twelve

in a few months, but isn't all this kind of stuff a bit

adult for us?

So, message for today, do not pull your winkle out

Boys because you may end up screaming like a

lickle ittle

ittle little girl, and if you're lucky youll go off with

a hole in your hand and not your...DICK!!!!!

Hahahah I best refrain (good word, looked it up

on google) from such swear words, in case my nan

one day sees my blog...anyway, one of them days

I suppose because I want to be honest.

As much

as I loved bake off on bbc1 the change to channel

4 has me hating on that scary looking guy and

that tiny midget woman, that my nan always calls

a "pompous dyke!" I was like, "woah nan!" and she

was like, "I am not homophobic, but she is a

pompous dyke!" woah, what is it called, sour

grapes much Grannie-oh.

Also , I got to admit something, I am in love with

chloe grace moretz and I can admit this, as you

know, daisy isn't my real name, to keep up my

anonymity (I had to respell that like ten times,

uhhhhhhhhhhhh, dull!) is hot, HOT HAWT so hot,

she is feisty and very pretty, and Dorey, my friend, she

is black, and is into all that LBGTQ plus stuff, told

me about a film she was in, and I watched it with

her, and then Dorey told me she touches herself

over it…

I didn't know what she meant until she showed me

her non-eee, and started playing with that lumpy bit

we have that is called a clit…

for clitoris that is…and it made me feel all

strange. And then I realised that I am a dyke, as, I

felt something seeing Dorey's noonie, I know, I

know, I shouldn't as my nan tells me being gay is

worse than being black, which, ohmygod imagine

if nan knew that the "darkie" I was hanging

around with was also a "lesbo!" good god she would blow the heck, oh lets write up, the fuck up!!!!!!

I know this stuff is a bit adult, and boys getting their dicks out (ooo there I go again!!!!) seems a bit much, what is wrong with two girls showing off their bits and discovering new things?

Dorey told me she wasn't ready for the big leagues, and I asked what she meant, and she said porn... but, I feel really low, all of a sudden, because, well, she, my Nan that is she hates "darkies" and "gays" and, one day I hpe she reads this, so she can better understand how much it upsets me...

my nan is my only family, my bitch of a mum left me age two weeks, for some hippie "junkie" in my -

nans words, to go play "string instruments and

blow their heads off on drugs!" (SEE ABOVE IN

MY OLD BLOG POST ABOUT MY FAMILY TREE
AND

HISOTRY, where it is all about me, me, me, me,

and she, that is my Granny) – but I really do not

agree with the things she says, and it upsets me I

have to be in the house with someone I so love

but have to accept because she feeds me and

looks after me and "keeps me fed, safe and

sound" her corny words, not mine, like DUH!

It confuses me, and it gets me angry, that when I

hear it, recently she has been telling me there is

something different…yeah no shizz, you are a

homophobe and a racist, so Dorey tells me, and I

looked it up, never wanting Dorey to know I know

little, and am not much of a reader, I am too

invested in Zoe Sugg, Jenna marbles, Ingrid

Nilsen, michelle pahn, KSI, who is hilarious and

has the funniest laugh EVER!!!!- pewtiepie used to be so hot, but now he is not, he is like so annoying, and all those

beautiful influencers... online... I am a subscriber,

they are everything I should be

and want to be just like them, but, with my own

mode of cool, sexy, though I have yet to grow any

boobs and my lips look like dried out raisons, but

when I start to mature ill be sure to be like that!!!!!!

I will be sexy, though so many girls are already

looking ready to go to "court" and have a shag up

a back-alley wall, I dont want to have sex, I just

want to bloom, like a sparkly unbelievable flower...

every time I said this Dorey would say, "you girl

are going to be deflowered the way you doing at

that thing!" after we had one of our girl gossip touch

ourselves below night… pointing at my sore clit.

Sooo oh, guys, it is one of those days, one of them days, my nan says,

when her back hurts, and the other day, when she started on about Paul o grady, the dog mad guy on ITV1 , calling him a "fairy" and his voice was like "nails to me brain, like a chalkboard, bleeding poof!!!" I said to her, "oh one of them days is it again nan?" and she looked at me as if to say "you being smartass!" but she never said it, as I started to laugh, because I couldn't quite believe I said it, so she thought I was all like, "look at me, im copying my nan, my lovely fun, hilarious nan!" no, I was putting you down bitcha, like you put down others so pointlessly, and harshly.

So, like one of them days, I decided to confront

my nan the other day, and I asked whether she thought she was a racist homophobic (bitch!!!!!) She grunted at me and said, "only take issue because they're all wrong!!!"

after that, I had to decide, leave her be, she is old, bit like Catherine Tates Nan character, she is inappropriate and from like the medieval days, and just put it off as that, one of them days, or should I change one of them days, to when she would never ever say such a thing, so all I can do for her is excuse her behaviour, for one of them days, maybe if I could make it one of them rare days I can forgive her, but as I grow up, I realize I do not want to be like her. Bitter, vruel, oops, very cruel, and nasty.

So, maybe I should discount it as one of them days myself, where I am hating on my gran.

Anyway, that's enough for today guys, much love, and thanks to all ten people following me, you guys rock, and with you rocking, together we will become STARS!!!!!!

4. One of them Days *for Matthew Whyte, who thinks his neighbour is taking the piss.*

Dear neighbour, we have been this thing called, neighbours, for almost ten years now, and even though we nod, and smile, and wave, in that familiar way most neighbour's do, when they spot each other, we're both too busy to stop for one minute, to actually exchange numbers or information, where we can arrange a date to meet up, chinwag, or **"shoot the shit!"** as they say in good old America- (I mean what a mess that all is, right? With Trump?! And if you're sympathetic to the Trump way of life, with all that MAGA bullshit, maybe burn this in hate)- and I feel this is rather sad.

Because I wish nothing more than to have some form of basis, so I can measure what is the right tone to take, when tackling this certain issue, that I have, with you.

Yes. You. Only you. Not your dog.
 Not your wife. YOU.

I wish I had some form of bond or to have some form of link to you, so I can go in wholeheartedly and spew my guts out, over the subject of this nicely typed out message.

I believe, by having not formed any actual neighbour-ly bond or engaged in any conversant form of communication – for either one of us to be able to make a measure of a man, in our own separate ways, for us to make an opinion upon what kind of men we are. It is a difficult one. The likes of which you can apply to myself.

But, since being let off work these past few weeks, due to Covid-19, I've noticed something and had time to look around me and notice the finer things that work hides from me as I get out the door, with early rays and breeze helping me sip delicately at me thermos of black coffee (ten sugars, might I add, and yes, ten sugars you might say in astonishment, well guess what "buddy" I fucking well need it).

A wider world of chores. That my dear wife does for me, alongside the thermos she brews up for me, and of whom has to do such chores and things, that, as already mentioned before, I am sheltered from doing, due to my early morning wake-up call and duties, as the main breadwinner, I have no time to study my surroundings, of my own property.

So, my wife, these past two weeks, has time to sit back, as I familiarise myself, not with my neighbour's, which you may feel I should do with this time given to me, but as I've surveyed around me, you are a hard man to pin down and get a hold of, but also, after the recent revelation offered to me, I don't think I would want to.

I've decided, I need to be a stay-at-home type, if this period elongates any further due to this awful, awful virus, I need to adapt.

So my lady love deserves a lay in and for me to take upon these household, and outside-hold duties; such as going out and doing the stuff she does, after I drive away to work, to be faced with something, that requires her to bend over, who has a bad back, yes, a bad back, my lady love, my wife, of whom has to, must bend over to "collect" your dogs shit! My poor wife! Isn't it enough with her bad back, man? And a lady with an overly sensitive gag reflex on the best of days, I might add…oh ho, I should know, as a BJ has never existed in this household, I am telling you…- or risk having vomit gushed all over you, sir. All of this, on top of everything else, to bend down, to pick up your dog's shit… first of all, who the fuck do you think you are, mate? And secondly, why?

Why do you let your dog out for his morning shit ON MY FUCKING GRASS-verge! Onto my front garden bit!

The front yard part, yeah, my green, my verge, that you do not need your dog waddling over, with much encouragement, near my driveway, and my front porch, but, if I wrote yard, I'd sound like a twat, but if I don't, a lot of us Americanized Brits, part of this current generation, of whom are confused as to what country they live in and how best to pronounce certain words and associate things and terms-wouldn't understand, when directing you to the part of my property, that you let your DOG shit on.

CONTINUALLY!

I stopped myself from reacting so dramatically, so I have waited, over the next few days, surveying your happenings before you end up dressed to the fucking nines, and shoot off to work.

Away from the steaming pile you left-there, from what I can guesstimate as being shoved out into this glorious well-tended verge of mine not ten minutes before you fuck off to work with your limp handed usual wave.

(Are you saying farewell to your dog's doo-doo? Think it is funny? Got a dog poo fetish, like to see it steaming away like a furnace in your rear-view mirrors?)

You receive and get in reciprocation a full-hearted well-meaning one, a well-intended wave, from myself, not knowing that behind me is the biggest pile of shit I could ever imagine coming from such a small, beautiful little dog.

How much does your veterinary bills cost, for anal reconstruction surgery for the poor little fuckers' poop-chute?

Yours, the wave that is, it is… well, it stinks, so much I mention the limpness of it, even my wife starts to gag, it's that sickening (like I said, she has an easy and sensitive gag reflux)… it stinks, like your shitty attitude - to the high heavens as a fake reciprocal gesture- that you afford me. I waved with gusto before I realised what type of man you are. Now I'll just flip you the bird.

You are a lazy fucking cunt!

Pick it up. Bin it! Simples.

Got enough time for your sweet little doggoh, to come trotting onto my property, taking a massive shit (what you been feeding it? The other neighbour's pets? Oh, yeah, that's right, there are not any pets bar your own on our street) - a shit that must take a while to process and come out of that animal's little poop hole. In that time, why not, um, get a bag, pick it up, keep with you so you may have all day good fucking luck.

Two weeks I've watched you. Two weeks, I have waited, in hope that it was just one of them days and you're just a bit off.

Nah, you're off 24/7 Sonny-Jim!

 PICK IT THE FUCK UP!

 From your neighbour, across the way, with his well-intended wave, or affirmative nod.

The guy whose grass verge you let your dog crap in!

Hope to see no dog shit on my property come the morning, best wishes, The Stronger-Handed-Individual, Matt Whyte- your dog's ass much?

A few days later, there was an unexpected knock on the door.

Timid. Apologetic.

To Matthew Whyte's ears, that is me, and my own ears - this was the day.

The day of reckoning.

No dog shit, yet no apology.

I waited.

Nada.

Nothing.

Now, 6:35pm, here they come. I knew it, I just knew it was going to happen. Not of his own volition.

As I open the door, there is his wife, whose obviously dragged him over, against his will.

The guy had a look on him, of genuine, unconcernedness.

He might as well have been a teenager, dragged across the road whilst his iPhone was in tow, ore interested in chatting to his dimwitted mates, as he was forced to apologise for being a bratty little bitch.

That was what this guy exhumed himself, without having the added acne, the BO taint, and that certain brand of hoodie most teens own at some point in their life, with that drawn out, almost drugged look about them even though they've probably never even tried drugs let alone smelling bath salts, and they all have a perpetual dosser-gormless-ness about them.

He exhumed worse.

Arrogance. Assuredness. A man who suffers no consequence for his actions.

Add insult to injury his wife brought the, oh so cute little pup, big eyes, droopy eyes, panting away, probably needing another humongous shit, half its size, that she jiggled and used its paws, that she made it wave and then put together in a pitiful attempt to beg for our forgiveness.

After much nudging, and cough, cough, ahem-ing, the spoilt man-child looked up, rolled his eyes...ACTUALLY ROLLED HIS EYES IN FRONT OF US, and stated,

"Look, I am truly..."

"Sorry, yes, sorry, aren't you, I mean, he is so busy and stressed at work, right hun? Right?" his blonde bimbo wife butted in.

Now I can half understand why the guy doesn't try to talk.

Nah, I am being unfair, she is trying her hardest because she knows, better than anyone, trying to get a genuine, hand on heart apology from him was like getting warm blood from a cold-blooded creature.

This guy couldn't give two flying fucks. He just couldn't. Not one fuck was given in the way he held himself.

No eye contact!

Nothing.

What are you, autistic?

Oh, yeah, I bet if given a chance you would use that and apply it to yourself, though you are the sort who refers to his "clientele" as retards for not taking the offer or deal you had so masterfully executed for them.

No autistic person would do that. I am sure of it.

Cunt.

Do not try that on me son, I am a Dr.

You're just an arrogant *boy* and feel everyone is beneath you.

Also, I have done my work on you, boy, oh yes I have, you sell cars for a living,

I sell nothing. I heal people. Go suck an exhaust pipe you...

"It has just been one of those days!" – blonde bimbo states, nodding between me, my wife, for some odd reason also to the dog, then back to her partner/husband/bit on the side-that-she-lives with-whatever the fuck!

Fuck. The. Both. Of. You.

"Yeah, its been one of those...*weeks!*" he stretched out the word *week* so far that we almost reached the end of Sunday which was four days away.

So, all his wife's apologies, waffling, on his behalf, and excuse making, went in one ear, out the other.

I wanted to hear it from him. But as soon as she said that, well, I was ready to blow, then he jumps in.

With that, of all excuses, for such a blatant disregard for his neighbour's and fellow man's property... I WAS READY.

Luckily, here enters my wife,

"More like one of those years!"

Too right. Blame it on your mind-frame. It being one of those days. One of those weeks, or months or years…

"Yeah, like I said, its been one of those…"

Say weeks, I dare you!

 My mind is screaming. I am seething by this point. I should have started to froth at the mouth, and apologise it away, as it had been "one of those days…"

Was that a smile, did he just have the audacity to look down, blushing? Faux bashfulness?

"Like I said…"

He looks me dead in the eyes.

"It has been one of those. . .*lives*!"

****

"Well, that went well" I said, seating myself down, having spent a night in a police cell, happy to have been there no longer than an hour and a half.

"For whom, exactly?" the wife said,

"Me, of course. Lucky Harold was on tonight, otherwise it would have been much longer."

Harold is one of my patients and knows I am not a violent man, also, Harold went to buy a car off this toss-rag before and he pissed him off to no end.

Nepotism? Not really. A pricks a prick. A favour is a favour. I just prescribed him a longer dose of his pain meds than is necessary.

"That man has four front teeth missing and an eye-socket swollen out like…"

"Like their dogs' asshole" I quipped.

The wife responded with an arm punch.

"What were you thinking?" she settled next to me, all forgiven, as I can tell she thought it was a rather hilarious tale, that I know she will use for next week's book club.

"I don't know, hun!" I winked down at her.

She squirmed.

Bless her.

"I think it might just be…*one of them days!*"

5. One of them days... *for Seamus, the seabird (or is it Seagull?)*

*Food. Flap me wings. Swoop down. Wind. Air. Plummet. Cannon ball. Flap them. Meeeeeeeeowwwwwwwwwwwwwahhh. Not like a cat. Fuckers like to think they can get big old Seamus. Seamus the Seaguuuuuuuuuawawawaawawawawawrkarkark! Meeeeeeeeowwwwwwwwwwwwwahhh, like the airplanes high above me. My cousin Ralph got caught in one of their propeller thingies. He died. As did everyone on that plane. The life of 235 for the life of one seagull. That is good odds, Awrk! Awrk! Awrk! Awrk! Awrk! Wark?! I'm a little seabird, short, not stout, here is my wingtip, here is the grout, caught between my webbed talon-things, tweet, tweet, tweet, fuck those sweet birdies, with their song, it makes no sense, and is all wrong, wrong, wrong. Grace. Speed. Velocity. Wingspan. Tuck in. Deep dive. Wooosh! I am a rather imaginative seabird, ain't I just? Which Lesser-Blacked-Back Gull do you think can think like me? Who do you think I am? I am no Glaucous Gull nor European Herring-Gull, not since this Eat Brexfarst thing. I am me. Seamus. Sea is in my name. **Sea**mus. So, none of this Larus argentatus, Larus marinus, Larus fuscus, Larus glaucoides – stuff! I am Larus Brightonius! I am a new Larus Magnifique-tus-us!*

I am an independent, new type of bird. So important I am, do not even bother pronouncing the B! I am an New-Age Indie-Lesser-Is-More-Black Non-Herring-'ird! Watch me soar. Watch me fly. Watch me eat. Caw. Shit. Splat your car as if I have a vendetta against you. That I do. That we do. I cannot talk much upon my seagull brethren, as, they're dumb as mustard dried out on a nasty sweet brioche bun. Sweet buns and tasty mulched meat and mustard and that red sauce called Ketchup-pleeease, you must take me for some amateur seagull. I have taste, man! Though I may have a Gammy leg, I am a strong independent gull. I have a cloaca to make most of the other sweet-lady loves want me. Due to my mutation, my sexual organ is a bit on the long, and droopy side, and in all honesty, its weird as most other seagulls tried to tear it off me, as if something to eat. Though my cloaca is different, it still shouldn't be subjected to such abuse, just because its more, um, cock-like, is that the human word for their tally-whackers we used to go for sometimes, before we learnt what they shot out of it - on the sandy beaches of, wherever there are sandy beaches(?) - in this bipolar weathered island. Parental duties are always divided between us and I do not want to hear anymore negativity or derogatory comments upon us. Think we ain't listening to you as you watch us procreate and then nurture our eggs then young? Do not be fooled, Seagulls are smart. We just, act dumb out of our birdy-bestiality – is that the right word? I mean, caw! Caaaw! Doesn't quite cut it for this current situation. Every time I show any interest in that huge book, that tastes good when it's sodden and wet, people shoo me away or just laugh. I am an educated bird, so stop it, alright! Stop judging me by my size and Where was I? Where am I? In, East Sussex somewhere, though Brighton, Hastings, Eastbourne, they all look the same to me. Shitholes. Caw! Caw! Haaaaaaaaaaaaaaawrrrrrr! Not so much grace or tactility there right, fellow Brightonian's? Laridae in the suborder Lari, was where we herald. Not me. I am a BriGull! Where am I now? Oh, right. Flight. Light. Sea-salt. Scabby leg. Limp leg. Is it a leg? Fuck it. What do these humans say, YOLO. You only like oysters. I wish! Nothing decent on this here beach but leftover takeaway cartons and the fish that manages to surface for long enough for one of my brethren to swoop down take a nip and realize, yuck, this fish tastes like actual fish and they discard it. All because it ain't covered in the red stuff. And it isn't slippery, like, Earth-made slippery, I mean, human cooked kind of wet, and, well wet, whilst wetly mildly warm, oily-ark-ark! Sorry about that, though I am not your average minded bird, sometimes the bird cannot help but to caw! Caw! Caw! Nor salted, either, to think upon it, normal fish sucks. Maybe I am a bird of a refined and developed taste...I love the batter-sea stuff on it, crunchy, and covered in breadcrumbs, but from those packets in finger formation, with that Pirate looking gimp on the front of the cardboard packaging, that no matter my intelligence and awareness, I still peck at and gulp down, then get confused as to why a whole package is obstructing my chest and my maneuverability. Oh, if only I could salivate I would, instead I'll make my still baby-seagull obsidian eyes go a bit rounder, flush up my feathers – and look cute. I'll still eat it. I know what I am. A gannet. Where am I, oh, look, a lamppost is coming straight towards me. I wonder, maybe if I just, well, time it right, I may not impact so hard, and actually collide, not to risk death or disability, as I do not think Seabirds like me can claim on disability allowance – as I make out I am about to fall as a broken-necked gull. Slowly falling. Dramatic. Cinematic. Yes, pigeons roost in old theatres and cinemas, as do I and so do I, so just leave it out, okay? I just, kind of, walk in whilst everyone is getting all frenzied over some film with a scary looking creature all furry like a dog (shivers) and a blonde woman wielding a blue stick with a masked badass behind her, waddling between them, occasionally speaking their lingo, just to throw them in their already hyper mania, and ensure I get a few toffee sticky popcorn bits, that sticks to my puffed-out breast, to chew over as I watch those arthouse films about cars, guns, and doves. Nerds, I heard one blonde refer to them, as she cued up for a film by a ginger woman, that upon reflection is always in The Sun newspapers, I love that paper, houses the best fish and chips ever referred to as The Freckled Hot Mess nobody cares about, Loony Longhands? They all end up coming out complaining, what do you expect, you're at a Curzon cinema, quality and high class, aye! Aye! HAWKR!!!!!! Sorry, swallowed a fly. You want to watch art? Go see the re-run of a John Woo film, like I do. All that slow motion man, and the doves, fuck, I want doves to just appear in and around me as I fall to my potential doom! See me....ohhhh, ahhh, my gosh, poor wee seagull...as I am falling... as a dead weight – though one must ensure there is a form of cushioning below me, so when I land, A: I do not die, B: don't go out of this Earth looking like an even bigger nit-of-a-bird-tweet-tit! I can jump up, wings spread-wide and go "Ta-DAH!" mocking every seagull that ever flew to see the end of a day. I do this just to test my perception. I do not break my neck, I swerve it. If other seagulls had a modicum of awareness they'd appraise such aero-gull-dynamics. Anyway, where was I? Oh, yeah, the bird in me is getting more prolonged, I keep losing focus, I see food, I gotta get it! **OH LOOK!** *Food, in human hands. I am a smart enough type of Gull to go down there on me todd and take it off the lardass.* **GONNA GET IT, GONNA GET IT... WHAMP! Ouch!** *Ooooofah! Bastard just punched me in the beak. I'll give him a surprise. Quack! "Huh? WHATTHEFUCK?!" Yeah, that's what you deserve. A seagull quacking. Oops, squark! FOOD I just popped my gull-hole. At least it was in a public space, as the other gulls are always looking at me critically as if to say, "Why do you not shit on them from up above" that is, if, like me, they had the capabilities to talk, let alone think, they wouldn't. No, actually they would. Because they're ordinary birds. Dirty bastarrrrrrrks! I just do not like pooping from a great height. I always feel like I need my legs planted either side of me, but I cannot even do this, oh how I wish I were knock kneed like Mr. Perry, the only human who feeds us the good stuff.*

Mr. Perry also has an utter evil contempt for pigeons. Those slow-paced little dumplings, always jutting out there heads in some cocksure fashion.

Which transposed onto a human, you'd think they're either A: Tourettic or B: fucking stupid and like to say words like Bruv and Fam! What was this hate really about? Well, I will tell you, no one in particular... "Pappa Bird can you hear me? Can you hear my squark, CRY!" - because he used to rear them and then some day they got an outbreak of a disease and it spread to both bird and his wife. Killed his birds, pigeons mostly, and also killed his wife. Didn't care for his wife much. Just was annoyed he lost out on many hundreds of prized pigeons. This information was so compelling. Just think about it. Well, my fellow bird friends can't, as they can't think. Which they don't, but, aha, I do. But the issue with a Gull like me is, you may walk like me, not caw! - like me, you may swing like me, but you will never be me...The issuuuuuuuuarkarkarkark! Sorry, thing is, I am bird, so the bird like part of me always corrupts the, what I can only assume is the seagull-self of me, that part that it ain't human, but with what only humans can equate to being their ounce of sense and self-awareness, I can only state, that "humanity" in me, makes everything go a little which way, that is so I am more human than bird, but more bird than human. With all these thoughts and notions, and analyses, the bird like spasticity, and oscillations and mechanization of our thought processes, mostly our instinct to EAT FUCK BATHE and occasionally sleep on rapid waves, for your average bird this is, well, um, er, Awrk!-

WARD! THINK SEA-MUSS, tink! Tink! Tink! Um, well, like, it would see them like, blow up...the seagull that is. I am no terrorist-bird as I am too free for all that shit, getting caught by a terrorist to be then be used as practice for their weird blowing up vests. For me, it is like, corrupting a human type hybrid form of thought, so I am a bit of a personality even in the world of both bird and human. Seagulls are self-aware. They're just not prone to being all that reflective or not in want or is it won't? - to do such things. They eat. Drink. Water themselves. Salt water. Barley water. Piss water. Beer. Bin juice. Bathe. Shit. Shag. Caw, a few times a day. Simples. We have no reason to be the noisy assholes we are, but we are. We are making a stand. Only, I am the one who is aware of it as being something revolutionary because these type of gulls, do not know what they do. Today, is one of them days. I do not know what this means, but Mr. Grumbles, another bird feeder, said it, when he struggled to unclasp the feed from his hand. Unapologetically we all swarmed in, not giving a fuck we were chomping more of his flesh than bird feed, but fuck it, at least I had the nous to apologise after. And since then, ever since we nigh on nearly killed him...I say, to any bird, or person listening, if I think they're having a tough time of it... "Its one of them daaaaaaaaaaarks!"

6. One of them days, *for Tony to kick back, and reflect upon America.*

Oh say, can't you see...I cannot remember the rest, I just simply can't for the life of me. 56 years old and my memory is worse than a shot liver. Which I already got. My words too do not seem to get along. 58 years old and I am terrible with everything. I drink enough water and beer and club soda's to be deemed legally healthy-ish. I love my country. 68 years old I am.

I love my guns. Just, thing is, I cannot remember where I put them.

The speeches, well, well, they I have in my head.

Wanna hear my favourite of them, from America's finest President, nope, not that second best, that is Trump, but the best of the best. George W, Bush.

"When they struck, those terrorist sonsofbitches, they wanted to create an atmosphere of fear, and one of the great goals of this war is...to tell the traveling public: Get on board. Fly anywhere you want. If they try anything, sacrifice yourself like the good American you are. Fuck those sumbitcheups! Do your business around the country!
Fly and enjoy America's great destination spots!

If them - terrorists are there, hijacking, just point them out, these true American landmarks, and make them realize, you do not want to destroy this!

By all means, fuck us up and crash our plane!
But not bomb or fuck up that location, as that place, is industrial and capitalist owned property!

And my hand has a lot of stake in that business, not yours, but your good friend George Wilheim Bush! All of it, being blown up! What is it good for? Many businessmen, of whom I have a share in their business. So, hit select approved zones will yah? Get down to Disney World in Florida. If you cannot get there, ensure those terrorist bag on the head types, with our guns, and our training, to crash-land there, so when you die, you die knowing, at least you ended up in your intended location. Who can say then that the terrorist took away young Paul Studdles Make a Wish dream away from him. Take your families and enjoy life the way we want it to be enjoyed."

Amen George. Amen. The fear he saw in his face when it was told to him the Trade went down... as he was reading that story to the school kids.

Fear. Fear that was faced. No gulp. No adam's apple of W. Bushes went bobbing up and down in anxiety.

It was excitement. WMD finding time!

YEEEEHAW! Oh boy, it is one of them days, that I wish I knew where my gun was, so I can pop a few in the air in celebration of my happening to have one of 'dem days of reflecting and lovin; my country.

"Nixon, I lav you! You're not a crook!" my wife Darlene shouted from her bed.

"Darlene, shut the hell up!"

"Why should I?"

"Its one of dem days, WOMAN! I am reflectin'!"

"Oan whut?!"

"My favourite Presidents speeches!"

"You remember Nixon's last speech!"

"Honey, I basically wrote that muthar-fucking speech, wanna hear it?"

"Go for it, as it is one of dem days!"

"Right! Good evening. This is the 37th time I have spoken to you from this office, where so many decisions have been made that shaped the history of this Nation. For good, and for bad, and for the sake of recording my voice because I love the sound of it. Each time I have done so to discuss with you some matter that I believe affected the national interest. Like locusts in my back yard. That time Al Capone gave me a venereal disease just by talking to me down the phone.
In all the decisions I have made in my public life, I have always tried to do what was best for the Nation. Or for my own biased agenda.
Or, well, um, I am not a crook.

Throughout the long and difficult period of Watergate, I have felt it was my duty to persevere, to make every possible effort to complete the term of office to which you elected me. That you did, so remember, I am not a crook."

"I love that part baby!"

"Don't yah just, now, SHUT UP WOMAN AND LET ME FINISH! *Ahem*!"

"Clear your throat one more time baby, I wanna hear that spittoon of it go ooofffah!"

"Woman, do you wanna hear the rest or not?"

"Go ahead, baby, go ahead... *I am not a crook*...!"

"What yo say?"

"Get oan wit' it yah fat dumbass!"

"*Ahem!* In the past few days, however, it has become evident to me that I no longer have a strong enough political base in the Congress to justify continuing that effort. That and, I have always been, way in over my fucking forehead.

As long as there was such a base, I felt strongly that it was necessary to see the constitutional process through to its conclusion, whilst always sweating from my top tiered brow, onto all confidential papers, and remember, I am not a crook...

That to do otherwise would be unfaithful, which I have never been, all except that Capone scenario, which turn out, its wasn't even Capone... to the spirit of that deliberately difficult process and a dangerously destabilizing precedent for the future. Of which I moulded like clay in my own grubby hands. But I washed them in the blood of virgin olive oil. Monkey oil Okay, decent American oil stolen from the Arabs.

But with the disappearance of that base, my fan base, Hoorah! - I now believe that the constitutional purpose has been served, and there is no longer a need for the process to be prolonged. Meaning, I have out stayed my welcome, my American brothers, and sisters.

I would have preferred to carry through to the finish whatever the personal agony, like when, in the folds of my forehead, I get stress-blisters, right there, and the makeup department dots it with make-up, that makes it even worse...it would have involved such a thing, and my family unanimously urged me to do so, to leave before that blister burst on live television But the interest of the Nation must always come before any personal considerations, especially related to boils or skin diseases or infections.

From the discussions I have had with Congressional and other leaders, I have concluded that because of the Watergate matter, and that Hunter S. Thompson fellar, fucker, I might not have the support of the Congress, or the American man... That I would consider necessary to back the exceedingly difficult decisions and carry out the duties of this office in the way the interests of the Nation would require.
In my own self interests.

If there was a big red button, I'd be crooning over that thing 24/8, sadly, the FBI put that in, as a test.

It was a dummy. The real button is in the hands of a film director, called Stanley Kubrick. Kubrick, of whom, hoorah!- is most known for believing he directed the moon landings. This isn't so, I did that! In my back yard with aSuper-8 camera, yep, you better believe it, I am not a space-landing crook!

I have never been a quitter. Nor a crook, nor a crooky-quitter. Nor a quitter-y-jittery-crook.

I was so passionate about my degrees, I reset many, many exams, all questioning my state of mind, and I passed with flying colours. I was certifiably, insane.

To leave office before my term is completed is abhorrent to every instinct in my body, much like the time Al Capone visited me of Tuesdays and bathed me in his, weird, sexual drool. But as President, I must put the interest of America first. And myself, before all knowledge of my having thumped my hand down on that dummy red atomic nukes at the ready button YEEEEEHAAAAAAAAAR…"

"Honey…"

"Yeyup!

"Get on with it…"

"America needs a full-time President and a full-time Congress, particularly at this time with problems we face at home and abroad. That to which, I do not care. America rules. Hoorah!

To continue to fight through the months ahead for my personal vindication would almost totally absorb the time and attention of both the President and the Congress in a period when our entire focus should be on the great issues of peace abroad and prosperity without inflation at home. I want to be able to drink with no consequence to my mood. Currently, drinking is making me more unstable than usual.

Therefore, I shall resign the Presidency effective at noon tomorrow. Vice President Ford will be sworn in as President at that hour in this office. Lucky bastard that he is, he will also get my makeup crew. Who have done a fine job, hiding all my stress boils and blisters.

Whilst, also progressively making them worse.

As I recall the high hopes for America with which we began this second term, I feel a great sadness that I will not be here in this office working on my own, I mean...um, my, um ,your, the American people's behalf to achieve those hopes in the next 2 1/2 years. But in turning over direction of the Government to Vice President Ford, I know, as I told the Nation when I nominated him for that office 10 months ago, that the leadership of America will be in good hands. Better in others than mine, right? WRONG! I am not a crook!

By taking this action, I hope that I will have hastened the start of that process of healing which is so desperately needed in America. Though, said healing shouldn't have happened if it weren't for Capone...

I regret deeply any injuries that may have been done in the course of the events that led to this decision. Namely, I really fucked us didn't I?

I would say only that if some of my judgments were wrong, and some were wrong, they were made in what I believed at the time to be the best interest of the Nation. Or myself.

To those who have stood with me during these past difficult months, with guns pressed firmly in their backs, to my family, my friends, to Capones legal team, to many others who joined in supporting my cause, that's right, I am owning this, I am not a crook, my cause, because they believed it was right, I will be eternally grateful for your support. And for those back massages, especially on my forehead.

And to those who have not felt able to give me your support, let me say I leave with no bitterness toward those bastards, who have opposed me, because all of us, in the final analysis, have been concerned with the good of the country, however our judgments might differ. Sonsofbitches!

I pledge to you tonight that as long as I have a breath of life in my body, I shall continue in that spirit, selfishly and benignly, in however way such a man as Nixon can act benign. Pah, bullshit. I shall continue to work for the great causes to which I have dedicated throughout my years as a Congressman, a Senator, a Vice President, and President, the cause of peace not just for America but among all nations, prosperity, justice, and opportunity for all of our people. And for me. I liked recording my own voice and listening to it over and over.

There is one cause above all to which I have been devoted and to which I shall always be devoted for as long as I live.

When I first took the oath of office as President 5 1/2 years ago, I made this sacred commitment, to "consecrate my office, my energies, and all the wisdom I can summon to the cause of peace among nations unless they disagreed with me then I was going to fuck them up!"

I have done my absolute best, which wasn't much, considering, in all the days since to be true to that pledge.

As a result of these efforts, many all forehead itching related and mood enhanced, I am confident that the world is a safer place today, not only for the people of America but for the people of all nations, and yes, I'm looking at you, yes you, England, fuck you, you're shaped similarly to my head...and that all of our children have a better chance than before of living in peace rather than dying in war. That I , kind of, um, encouraged.

This, more than anything, is what I hoped to achieve when I sought the Presidency. This, more than anything, is what I hope will be my legacy to you, to our country, as I leave the Presidency. And, if anything, it was just one of them days, I guess. President Richard God Save him Nixon - August 8,th 1974 that was Darlene."

"Honey, America works off of that phrase."

"Darn tooting!"

"Baby."

"Yeah…"

"Say that one more time and I'll shoot you right between your sunken eyeballed face!"

"Darn…" - Shooting…commenced.

For Darlene herself, it was one of them days.

7. One of them days, *for Paul Stockton.*

Trod in dog shit. Dragged it halfway across London. Stinking up the underground. Stinking up my bus. Then my office. Then I had to go home. Boss made me. And still. After many miles. Many different transports. I still had remnants of it, and it stunk.

My wife had not left for work, herself yet. Getting an extra hour lie-in, as per was her usual.

I asked for assistance.

She turned her nose up.

Then hastened to work. Whilst telling me to dare not come into the house with them on.

They were multi-laced boots. They took an age to take off. And near impossible to slip off.

My only companion in this household was my dog, Shelly, and she caught a draft of the dog shit and turned tail.

I took myself to the shed.

At the end of the garden. Used the water-hose the other day to hose down an equally as smelly Shelly, who rolled in fox's shit, so I aimed for that.

As I turned the tap. It guttered. Spat.
Then...

 Nothing.

So, I go to inspect the water tank that takes rainwater,
and collects it, so I can reuse it, of course after
filtration. No water. *How odd. And it had been raining
last night. It is raining season.*

Then I spot it.

 Damn fucking...*um*, *animals*.

Chewing at the water tanks recycled plastic container,
on the corner, right on the edge. Looked like something
from a cartoon.

 My life is one big cartoon, just without any canned
laughter or general audience approval.

It's all winces. . . and groans.

I notice upon approach all of the water has flooded my
garden, around the water tank.

 It was too late to pull myself out, as I trudged to
inspect, it came up to my knees.

 I was drenched.

So, it seemed, it was going to be, one of them days.

You know the ones.

We all have them, and at the end of it, we all have a **sad sack of shit, ain't I just,** story to tell, at the end of it.

I could continue, but what is the fun in that?

You know how it ends.

More shit tumbled on me, physically and metaphorically, and before you knew it I was hospitalized with blood poisoning.

Seems in my haste to get my boots, and my trousers off, I scraped my thumb on the inside of the shed's door, that has a plethora of nails sticking out to greet you warmly by their stab.

One of them days, fuck me, isn't every day one of them days?

The End.

Well, not of that phrase or its meaning but to these selection of stories.

I hope they made you laugh, cry, giggle, or just look on at the page, perplexed as to what the heck you were actually reading.

That is my goal after all, to distract you from one of them days, you may be having, also, I wrote this whole book within about a day, give me a break –

Zak Ferguson,
11:38pm
17-12-2020
Eastbourne, East Sussex
(gagging for a smoke)

About the Author

Zak Ferguson is an Autistic, mental health-suffering, much despised entity. Barely a person, just an irritable itch, on the earlobe, on the fringes of your conscious-self, whose reality consists of words, literature and the pretensions garnered from art.

If you like literature that expands your perceptions of art, specifically within literature, that tests your patience, that entices, arouses, annoys, irritates, breaks into your machinations of consuming literature, try to read one or some of his books; that or at least if you want to try literature that confounds, upsets, and semi-forms itself as entertainment and all such and sundry as accepted and marketed in the full-fledged marketplace of book-building and publication ... Then Zak is probably somebody you'd like to beat around the head, with said book, and tell him what a waste of time it was. If, and this is a *BIG* if, this is an experience you wish to partake in, if only to get a chance to beat him publicly/privately, then read his stuff. Then get hold of him via zakferguson@hotmail.com

Zak lives in the seaside town of Brighton.

(He doesn't get out much)

(When he does, he is often told to go back home)

Printed in Great Britain
by Amazon